Verlag: BoD • Books on Demand GmbH, In de Tarpen 42, 22848 Norderstedt
Druck: Libri Plureos GmbH, Friedensallee 273, 22763 Hamburg
ISBN: 979-3-7597-9482-6

the GOLD BOOK

by: em Ritchie

—2024—

the Poltergeist

10·3·16

Six quills laden with black ink in a clear glass, the only impression when trying to remember.

First outside in sterile squares of designed gardens, then on the bedside table that used to lie under that painting of the two swans you made for me so many years ago.

In my old room, the one that never felt like home, the one that always felt invaded. It's sticky yellow, not my yellow. It's false promises of comfort.

I was lying how I always did in that bed, the one space of refuge I had. She came in uninvited, busying herself over some task-trying to be helpful but more so looking for a wound to conceal and patch over. She knew I was finally leaving and under the guise of helping me prepare for my journey away, she wanted to make sure she had left no visible mark that could ever be traced back to her injury.

I flew out of my bed, my feet never touching the floor, my form possessed and hanging awkwardly in the air. I flew over to her in the corner of my room, a scream in my chest and crazed look in my eye. Her head tilted back, her eyes agape and rolling back in her head, her mouth slightly open in shock, as I grasped her neck with my hands and tried to squeeze as hard as I could. I wanted to scream, you'll never hurt me again, get out of my room and never come back! But no words could come out. My possessed body just hanging slightly in that yellow room whose air had turned thick. We were caught there in that framed moment like time had turned to honey.

1

I wouldn't allow her to touch the things in my room anymore, to slowly replace them with her droves of sweaters that were all mild variations of the others, piling up and replacing my open space with her knitted neurosis. The feeling of dread palpable in my chest. In this room now I sleep in, in that yellow room; between the two I went, waking and sleeping in and out of, between them both. A gray form passed through the center of each and I watched it slowly, not knowing if the possession was from myself or from another outside dark force.

When I awoke in the yellow room again, I recoiled in horror to see her sitting on my bed. As I looked around the room, everything had been undone in my sleep-all of my coats were pulled out of the closet and lying in a pile on the floor, all of my posters were pulled off the wall and lying neatly around the edge of the room with their sticky rolls of tape exposed to the air. And as I glanced to the bedside table to the right I was filled with terror as I saw all of my colored pens lined up neatly with all of their caps taken off. Had my possessed form undone all of the things while I slept? Was there a ghostly poltergeist that rearranged my space as I slept? Or most eerie of all, did she come into my room and undo all of these things while I slept?

The inability to decipher what happened made me feel like I was starting to lose my mind, the room closing in on me, a panic rising in my chest. I dared not look at her in the face as she sat on my bed because I was sure I would see the face of a corpse, her eyes oozing and misshapenly shrunken in her skull, her lips falling off of her face, her skin putrid and purple.

After that moment a deafening infomercial blasted into the space, an effigy to help guard against the traveling salesmen who were forcing everyone to take pharmaceutical drugs. The scene of a wooden entry hallway to a house, seen from the perspective of a child from below, the doorbell ringing and the drug salesman pushing feverishly to enter the house.

Cut in infomercial speaker: Do you have those pesky drug reps foaming at the mouth to shove drugs down your throat? If so, do not fear, YARROW is available at your convenience just dial 888-647... A snapshot of a yarrow plume displayed emblazoned and twirling in the entry hallway.

At that I burst out of my bed past her clutches and ran into the rest of the house down the hall towards the living room. The house was completely dark except for the illuminated TV screen in the living room where he sat alone watching it in the dark.

In a panic, I tried to tell him what was happening but he was comatose staring at the TV, the yarrow infomercial blaring over and over on repeat on the screen. He was repeatedly turning the volume all the way up and all the way down, over and over, holding the remote out at the TV, staring blankly into the flashing light of the screen.

As I tried to scream at him about what was happening my voice became garbled and seemed to be controlled by the volume changer on the remote he was piloting.

In fits of sleep between two rooms they told me they were leaving and moving back to where they were from, to which I was confronted with feelings of relief but also of wondering what my home would be like without them there.

At some point I witnessed a group of highschool students being given their final year books before being turned out into the world, my stomach churning as feelings of revulsion for this sick conditioning ritual became clear to me. After breaking them down and molding them entirely, the students received a souvenir of their conditioning process to mark a final stamp on joining a societal reality that would eat them alive, that they never wanted to join in the first place.

At some point a red ape turned a swirling galaxy on a blue screen in front of him as he blankly stared at the television.

In the end I was trying to go to a conference on a subway system that was built deep underground, almost to the center of the Earth. I was completely lost and hadn't written down the address, I couldn't find the right train. I finally just decided to get on an arbitrary train, with a passerby telling me that sometimes you just have to pick a train to get on and then figure out how to get to where you're going after the train has already left the station.

The train car was elaborate and whimsical, with multiple levels of seating, a charming cafe, red diner window booth seats, a group of jazz musicians playing on some hidden corner and the most interesting assortment of creatures and people you've ever seen. A lit up half robot/half traveling banjo man, a pack of smoking intellectuals, a kind elder man with a pack of cards and a cup of hot chocolate. They all smiled at me warmly and knowingly, as if in on some secret joke that had a good ending. The train left the station and I watched the rolling countryside begin.

Seacraft
7·17·16

I walked slowly down the cool, winding sandstone stairs, they circled around to the left as the lamplight softly flickered and my fingers grazed the cracks and textures in the wall. My feet felt heavy. At the bottom of the deep stairs that seemed to go underground forever, a series of chambers unfolded, all filled with people who had lost their minds. Shrieking and inaudible violent murmurings reverberated off the deep blue sandstone walls. I caught a glimpse of a naked old woman, the fat of her body contorted and disproportioned, hanging off her form like melted tumors, slamming the top of her head into a wall over and over and over until her head caved in and her flesh was a pulpy mess to which the skin would reform and she would repeat the process infinitely. I walked past many of these chambers, each holding a tortured and isolated soul. At the end of the walkway I entered into a small, quiet, dark room on the right with no door, just a humble sandstone arch to make its entryway, my room.

I saw myself lying there dead on a cold, sandstone table slab. My skin was blue, my muscles taut and shrunken. I had laid there dead, alone for an eternity with no witness. As I gazed upon my dead body a bright orange flash erupted in my chest and my eyes snapped open, a gasp and cough on my breath. I sat up cold and alone, my body stiff and contorted. You were hanging there in the corner of the room, swaying slightly, your toes barely grazing the ground. Your form was white and rugged, like your edges were frayed or burned fuzzy. I never knew what your body looked like as it swung from some unknown crook in the ceiling. Was your face puffy and swollen? Was there blood running out of your nose? Were your eyes half open or half closed? Was your skin a faint lavender? Did your veins show through, were they a different shade of blue? Did your face look like a bloated corpse, was your mouth cracked open in an awkward silent scream? I've watched you hanging in my mind so many times but I never knew if the rope broke your neck or if you looked in pain or just looked forgotten. I unhinged your body from the unknown hanging crook and I carried you carefully to the edge of the river over my shoulder. You weren't even heavy.

I sat down with you next to the river in that lush green grass, almost the color of a rich watermelon rind. Our legs and toes were outstretched in the sun bobbing joyfully over the edge of the water. My long blond hair kept getting caught up in the warm breeze and you wore a cheerful beret as we ate strawberries and played with daisies. But in this sunny haze I can't quite tell the shape of the side of your face, or how your teeth were arranged with your lips, or the way your eyes caught the light. The tone of your voice is garbled, like it's only a faint impression you sent to me on the wind from far away. I am still struck by your wit and laughter, the care in your voice and in your eyes.

In my chest I am filled with a silent panic that your details have faded away from my memory and this best friend is now a hacked together series of gestures and images. I don't tell you this as we're sitting in the sun, reveling in our never-ending youth. I don't tell you I can't discern your voice or that last joke you sent hurdling at the sun.

I put layer upon layer of daisy crowns on your slight head, your hair is still so delicate and thin, your toes still so awkward and pale. I wrap you in a golden blanket flecked with periwinkle and I help you lie down in a small canoe. The river with its overhanging, jungly trees has opened up into the sea, streaks of orange and gold ribbon across the sky that creates an extended, eternal blue field where it meets the distant water. Your eyes are full of hope in the field of blue dreams and you take my hands softly to say goodbye before you step into the seacraft. There is a deep knowing as we look into each other's eyes that we will never see each other again. But our hearts are filled with lightness and excitement for your journey across the sea, even though the welling up of grief is palpable in my lungs.

You lie down wrapped in your blanket on the edge of the sea and I gently push you off the edge, yelling confidently I'll always love you and forcing a huge smile. I hold back my tears so you can remember me as full of joy when you think of saying farewell to a best friend.

I watch your seacraft get smaller and smaller on the dancing, colored sky. I sit on the lush grass next to the impressions of where we had sat together on the shore. I wrap myself in a silver blanket flecked with lavender and cry alone under the sun for an eternity.

Our Snowy Woods
8·29·16

It was late that one autumn evening when we returned to our blue forest under the swollen orange moon. The snow was falling early that year. White washed drifts nested in the tree boughs as we walked slowly down the path to our cabin by the glow of the night lit curves. Your warm hand found mine as I buried them both deep in my knitted coat pocket, the snow crunching softly and reassuringly under our feet as we walked. Your grin was soft and simple as we gazed out over the pine trees that were flooded with snowy blue blanket. The air hung like a milky cerulean dream. The snow gently swirled in the air like ashen fireflies. The silhouettes of the trees black, severe and all knowing.

When we saw the faint glow of orange through the snowy woods neither of us started to panic. Even when the frame of our hand built cabin brazen in flames came fully into view we didn't flinch or flicker with it. Its tortured, brash shape licking tendrils of crimson and electric orange into the deep blue sky, the ashen blue snow mixing in the ether with this psychotic blaze.

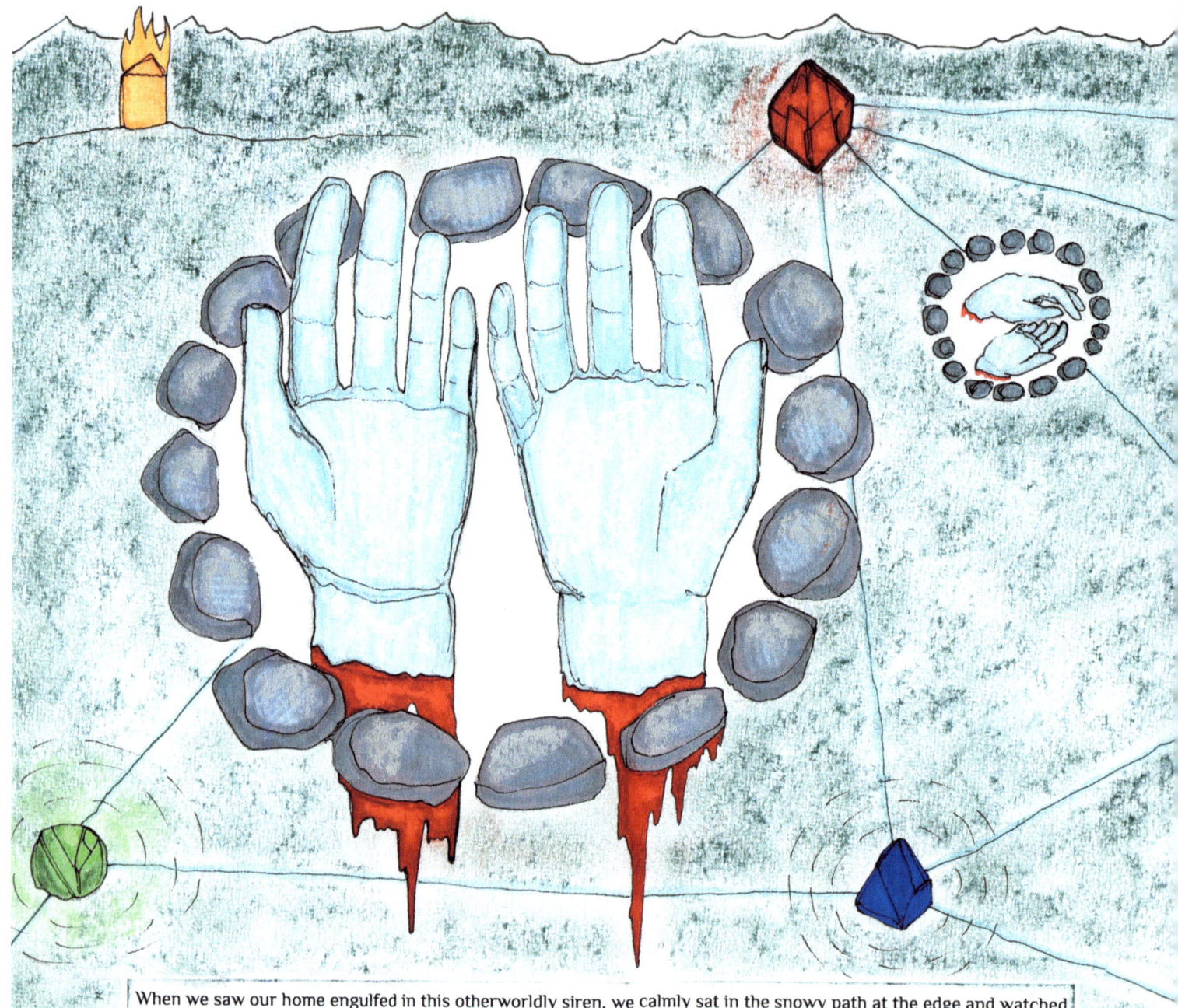

When we saw our home engulfed in this otherworldly siren, we calmly sat in the snowy path at the edge and watched. You in controlled measure began to cut off your extremities with such grace and precision. The blood ran hot in the white snow. As you trudged peacefully through the woods to find a place to bury your two hands and your two feet, I was confident that you would dig out the stone lined holes and bury your fingers and toes lovingly. For many years, you would travel every night into the dark, snowy, peaceful woods to unbury and rebury your hands and feet, the sunken and all knowing earth slowly purging all the memory from your flesh.

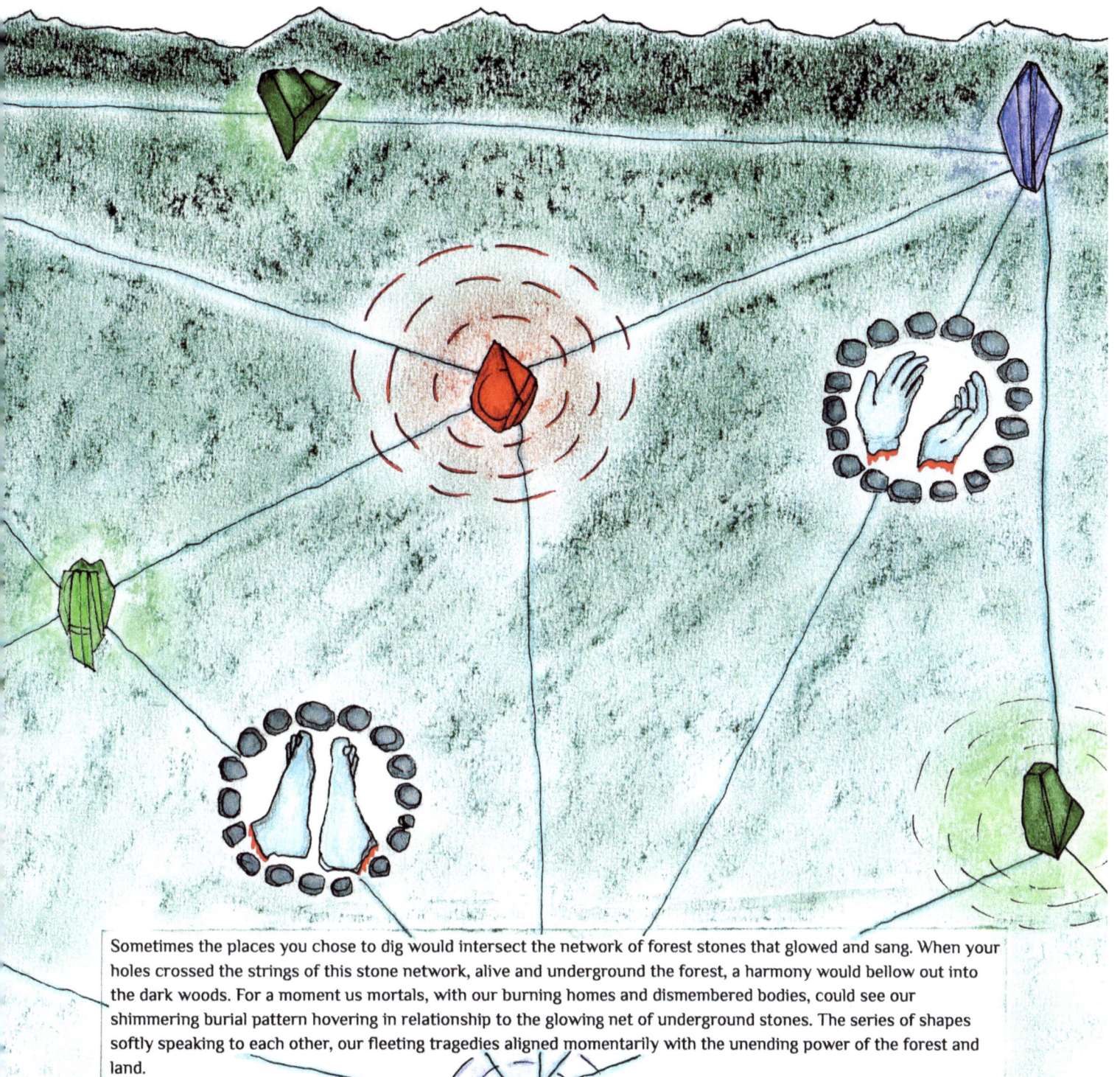

Sometimes the places you chose to dig would intersect the network of forest stones that glowed and sang. When your holes crossed the strings of this stone network, alive and underground the forest, a harmony would bellow out into the dark woods. For a moment us mortals, with our burning homes and dismembered bodies, could see our shimmering burial pattern hovering in relationship to the glowing net of underground stones. The series of shapes softly speaking to each other, our fleeting tragedies aligned momentarily with the unending power of the forest and land.

While you repeated this snowy ritual our home blazed bright, the skeleton of its form slowly disintegrating into electric orange sparks that tousled with the snow and the moon in the dark sky. Meanwhile, every night while you buried your hands and feet in different holes throughout the woods, I carefully removed my skeleton from my body and hung it from the loft rafters of our burning handmade home to be bleached white over and over again.

It was always night where we lived, so I was able to convincingly purify all the soot and blood and marks of sinew from my bones, the bell shaped rib cage gleaming and turning slowly as it hung from the ceiling. I watched my purifying skeleton dance like the slight mobile it was every night. I was comforted knowing you kept burying your hot limbs, letting them cool slowly and purposefully in the midnight violence of the rocks and soil's gifts.

After enough time my skeleton burned clean and your hands and feet remained in a frozen peace. The flames smoldered into the snow and in that dark pit of what was once our home we buried that swollen harvest orange moon. We touched palms as we disappeared, knowing we would never speak again. As our snowy woods faded from view, we knew it was irrelevant to ask if we ever mattered or not.

Underworld

Last night I was faced with the prospect of suicide, as I witnessed my life burning around me in the Death Valley desert and felt myself consumed entirely. There is nothing to say about the specifics of the catastrophe, the scale of healing required either a suicide or a visit to the underworld.

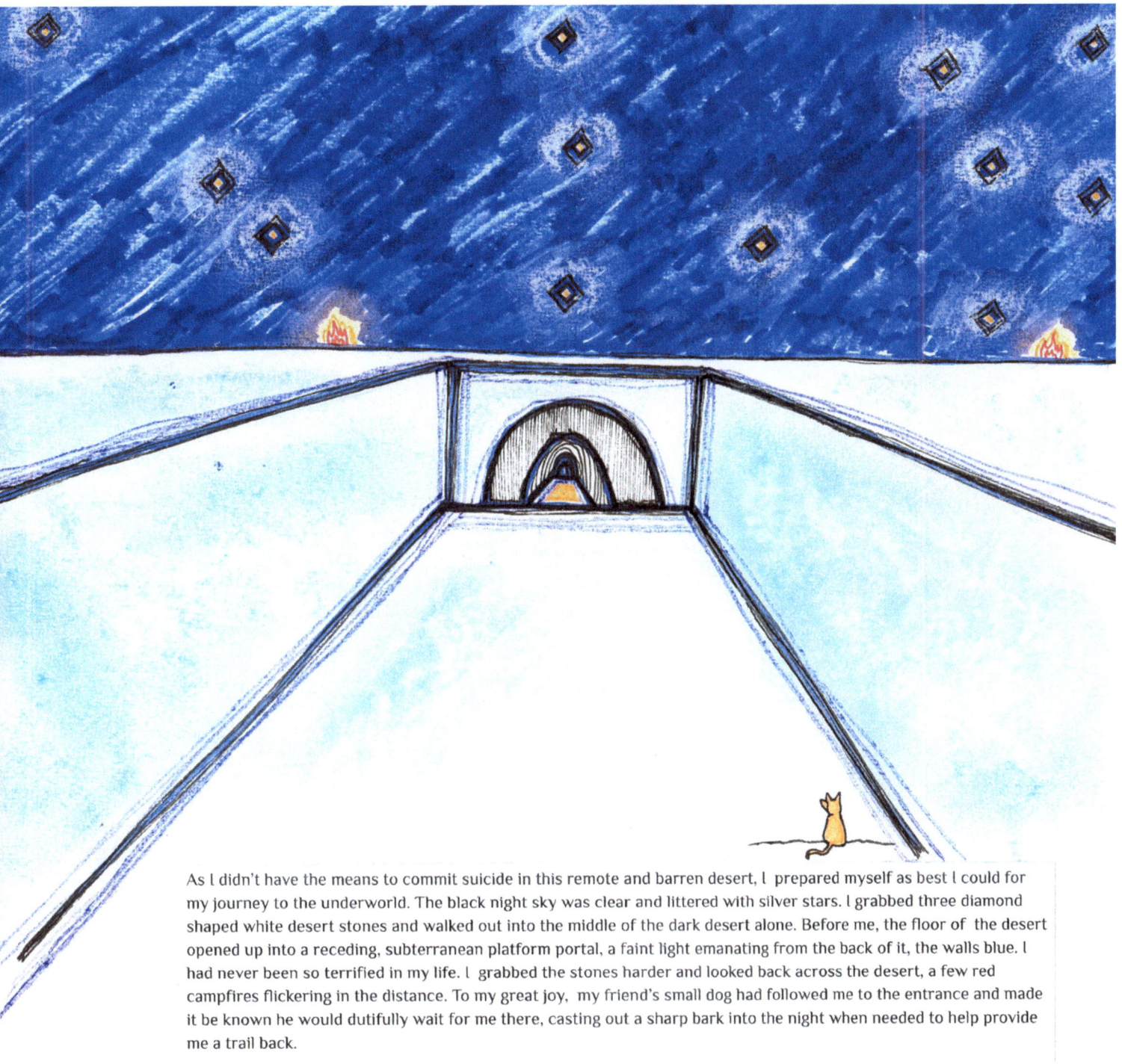

As I didn't have the means to commit suicide in this remote and barren desert, I prepared myself as best I could for my journey to the underworld. The black night sky was clear and littered with silver stars. I grabbed three diamond shaped white desert stones and walked out into the middle of the dark desert alone. Before me, the floor of the desert opened up into a receding, subterranean platform portal, a faint light emanating from the back of it, the walls blue. I had never been so terrified in my life. I grabbed the stones harder and looked back across the desert, a few red campfires flickering in the distance. To my great joy, my friend's small dog had followed me to the entrance and made it be known he would dutifully wait for me there, casting out a sharp bark into the night when needed to help provide me a trail back.

To my surprise, I was suddenly also accompanied by two giant black spirits with the bodies of humans and the heads of dogs. They flanked me on both sides, the one on the right with red glowing eyes and a more menacing demeanor, the one on the left with more human eyes and a reassuring presence. Before we embarked down the passageway, the guides prepared my body by making me appear to be dead. I was cloaked in white, my eyes and mouth blackened, my mouth filled with blood. I was terrified to see my own face as a dead one. They carved a steep line into the center of both of my arms, the blood running fresh, and also my shape into my forehead, cut deep into the flesh.

We began down the subterranean channel, but I was so paralyzed with fear it was hard to stay conscious, my steps somehow guiding me through fits of incoherence and insanity. As we walked, the horizon line of the desert became a series of bobbing triangular shapes that had the force of otherworldly beings. In the middle of this line, an abstract white and black lined shape began to form. Cries of pain and shrieks of insanity echoed constantly off the walls of the passageway. As we walked, I began to form this hovering shape into a wreath, its center adorned with two hanging pouches that I filled red with my blood. When we finally arrived at the bottom, millions of miles into the center of the Earth-into the otherworld, the underworld-we came upon a giant, midnight blue door, an enormous circular knocker cast in black iron towering above us. I hung my wreath on the door and knocked.

24

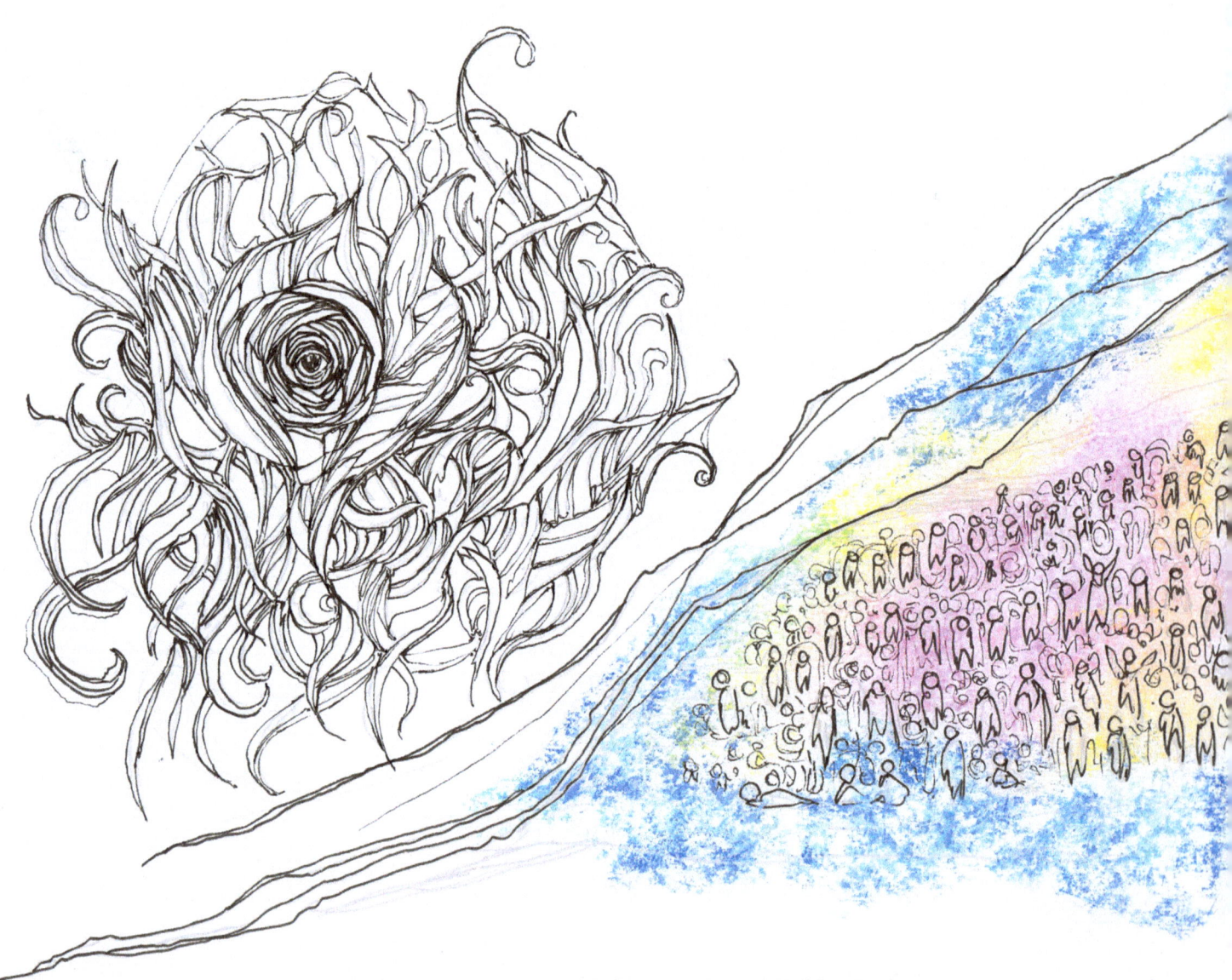

A small creature opened the door slowly, one wide, white eye peeking through a swirling mass of writhing dark tentacles and snakes that together en masse made its undulating form. It said nothing but its presence was not unwelcoming. We stepped in through the door, the air in the cavern thick and black, like black soot or black chalk pastel hanging everywhere. I was scared to even look around too much, I had heard the stories about people losing their minds or never returning from this place so I tried to keep my gaze unfocused.

I had no idea why I had been brought here, or what I was looking for, or how I would find the people and pieces of my life that I had been endlessly grieving. We stumbled on, following the gatekeeper's stride. At one point, we passed an opening into a much wider cavern that looked like it could've fit an entire world in its enormous chambers. In this giant cavern, ghastly pale colored lights flickered faintly on the walls-pastel pink, yellow, blue. The cavern was tiered into different levels and throughout the space a mass of heaving bodies and creatures were participating in an orgiastic scene, one of agony and bewilderment. Each of the tortured beings stuck in this cavern were alone in their individual plight or situation, the details of which were not clear. Together, the writhing mass created one contorting body that encapsulated the suffering of our world. Locked away forever in these chambers, with no witness to their plight, we moved onwards back into the thick blacken air, the scene closing behind us.

Mysteriously, after stumbling around in the darkness for some time, we first found him. He was contained in some kind of chamber with edges and walls made of the same blacken soot that hung thick in the air, as if the substance had its own intelligence and structure. It was as though the blacken substance in the air comprised everything in this underworld but at times made space within it to encapsulate and provide quarters for each tortured soul that was locked in its midst. My heart broke when I saw him, I had not been expecting to find him here. He first appeared as his young self, the brave and brilliant scientist who had trekked across the country to the Northwest to pursue his dreams of the forested mountains and all the intrigue and creativity present in a research based career. I saw myself and my sister as two little girls with him, we were happy and he was too, beaming with his dreams intact.

This scene faded to him sitting comatose and deadened in his chair blankly staring at the tv, the lights from the screen softly illuminating his frozen stare, the joy gone from his eyes, the life gone from his body. His body stiff, overweight, old and heartbroken. After his dreams in research were shattered by cruel and competitive colleagues, he felt forced to take a job that killed him inside. The only thing that momentarily relieved him of being crushed inside everyday at a job he hated was briefly numbing out his shattered dreams by staring at the tv or binge eating food; his soul taken and co-opted by the forces of capitalism-his generation in complete ignorance of depression. He sat locked in that chair and my heart wailed seeing him in so much suffering. I tried to call out to him but nothing could penetrate the black air, he couldn't hear me. I was consumed in tears.

What arrived next was unclear in origin-whether I had tried to muster up the most warm and loving memories I had with him or whether he conjured them into the space for me to see and remember-but I was flooded with potent and joyful memories of our time together, before his dreams were shattered and he died inside. Three memories more precious than any earthly substance of he, my sister and I: we are traveling in a canoe through the wetlands, we are sledding down a snowy hill in the mountains and walking through snowy streets in our neighborhood, we are sitting on the beach on that island and watching the comet Hale Bop in the glittering night sky. These memories rang clear throughout the air and filled me entirely with their sensations and feelings.

I was overwhelmed with tears of joy to be able to have these memories here in the depths of hell and for a moment I could see life flicker in his dead eyes. Whether I was instructed by him, or by the protector spirits, or from my gut, I gathered these memories as potent as I could keep them, miniaturized them as images and put them safely into a backpack that had appeared for my use. I strapped the bag on carefully to my back, making sure the memories were in there, double-checking and rechecking their presence in the sack. He faded from view into the black chalken air.

I walked onwards into the darkness and came upon her next. It was as if a long cell block existed, comprised of the black chalken air and she was in the room next to him without either knowing that they were both there. She, just like he had been, was dead and cloaked in an ashen blue, wearing all white-her skin pale and frosty, her eyes glazed over with a thick blue milk, pupils dilated, not focusing on anything. It was cold. She was frantically and hysterically running around her blacken cell, darting from one corner to the other, pounding on the walls, screaming, crying, drooling, stopping intermittently to shout something forcefully while waving her finger at the air- but all the words were nonsense, even though for a moment the loud directed tones she was making seemed to give her the illusion that she was sane or in control for a moment. Her tantrum continued endlessly, the edges of her becoming all the more blurred into a white chaotic form as she frantically raged. She also could not see me, for which I was grateful, as I was deeply terrified this crazed zombie may come for me.

Again, I was flooded by the best memories of her in this cold, dark space, but these ones took me more by surprise as I hadn't been able to remember any with her for a very long time. I was in the backyard in the old house picking bejeweled sap from the cherry tree while she was puttering around the kitchen inside. She was showing me how to tie my shoe and smiling in our old living room on the floor. She was giving me a small stuffed animal goose as I was falling asleep to help me feel better about something hard that had happened at school. She was telling me to change the channel about the nightmare I had where I was wearing the yellow duck raincoat and got hit by a car while crossing the street. She and he were throwing me an animal themed birthday party in our old house's backyard and my friends and I were all laughing as we played silly games with our stuffed animals. I was so struck by remembering these early, early memories I could barely breathe. Crying, I gathered them as quickly as I could into my backpack. I didn't know how long I could stay down here without losing my mind. She faded from view and I walked down the line.

The next chamber was larger, a small field of red lava rock with a zigzagging path in view, glowing lanterns dotted throughout the field. The black chalken air hung on the edges. Piles of clothes made tiny mountains, littered throughout the field. At the back edge the path culminated in the largest clothes mountain, atop which one of my best friends hung by her neck above it, the rope receding into the blacken ceiling into nothingness. I walked into this space and removed her body from the noose, gently carrying her over my shoulder. But when I reached the far edge of the field where the protector spirits stood her limp body became reanimated and flew into a crazed spasm. Her face was contorted and demonic, it didn't even resemble her.

Unlike the others, she was consumed in a red and violent hue, her eyes black and beady. I tried to calm her down, to talk to her but she was trying to kill me. The protector spirits snarled at her and corralled her back into her chamber. It became very clear I could not interact with or touch any of the dead and I had put myself in great danger in doing so. I was filled with a memory of being together in her apartment on the hill in Seattle, listening to music in the rain and laughing. I tried to conjure other memories but none came. Saddened and bewildered it was only the one, I put it in my backpack and continued on.

I kept walking down the line. In the next chamber stood the love of my life. He was numbly walking slowly throughout his chamber, clumsily bumping into the walls as though he couldn't see, to which I realized he had become blind. He looked so cold and alone, all cast in white, ashen blue with milky eyes. Seeing him there caused me to cry out and break down sobbing, the pain was too great. I called out to him over and over in a panic that I was right here and he wasn't alone. But he couldn't see or hear me. He wandered up to the edge of the chamber where I stood and I couldn't help myself but to plunge my hand in to touch his face.

As I did, he became flooded with a blue liquid, it ran down one side of his face and all the way down to the floor across his body, spurting from some inner fountain. As it did, it burned away where it touched his flesh, revealing his skull, eye socket and sunken teeth beneath. I screamed in horror and recoiled in pain, cursing his addiction as loudly as I could. I was flooded with two memories. We are on the stormy shore together on the Oregon Coast on our first trip together, laughing and shivering in the dark surf. We are on the beach on the channel on the far side of the island, looking out over the Olympic Peninsula hand in hand, huddling against the wind and smiling together, so in love, in peace. I carefully put these two memories into my backpack, the tears streaming down my face. I kept walking down the line, feeling numb and insane.

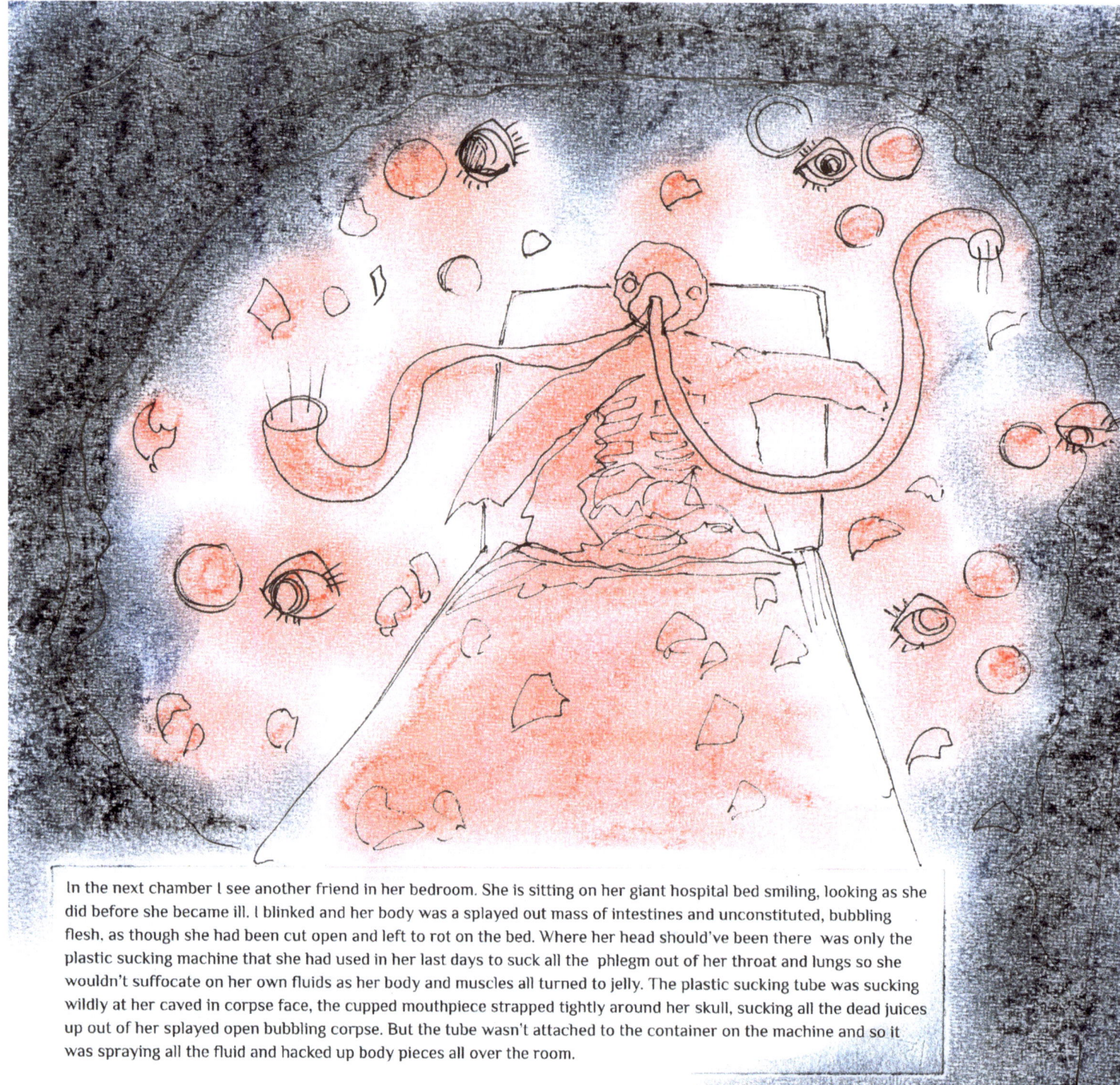

In the next chamber I see another friend in her bedroom. She is sitting on her giant hospital bed smiling, looking as she did before she became ill. I blinked and her body was a splayed out mass of intestines and unconstituted, bubbling flesh, as though she had been cut open and left to rot on the bed. Where her head should've been there was only the plastic sucking machine that she had used in her last days to suck all the phlegm out of her throat and lungs so she wouldn't suffocate on her own fluids as her body and muscles all turned to jelly. The plastic sucking tube was sucking wildly at her caved in corpse face, the cupped mouthpiece strapped tightly around her skull, sucking all the dead juices up out of her splayed open bubbling corpse. But the tube wasn't attached to the container on the machine and so it was spraying all the fluid and hacked up body pieces all over the room.

Some of the sprayed out pieces became her eyes, eyeballs floating throughout the space, blinking at me. The eyeballs were looking specifically at circles of color that also hung in the air, just as she had tried to communicate with us on that color coded circle chart with her eyes after our friend committed suicide and she couldn't speak or move anything but her eyes. I felt like I was going to throw up. I was flooded with two memories, the last times I spent with both of them. We are in their breakfast nook, the warm sunlight flooding the room and our warm breakfast of coffee and pastries. We are at the tea room having the finest tea, fit for royalty, tall layers of silver platters holding cakes and mini-sandwiches, they are smiling and laughing with me. I put these moments in my backpack and kept walking.

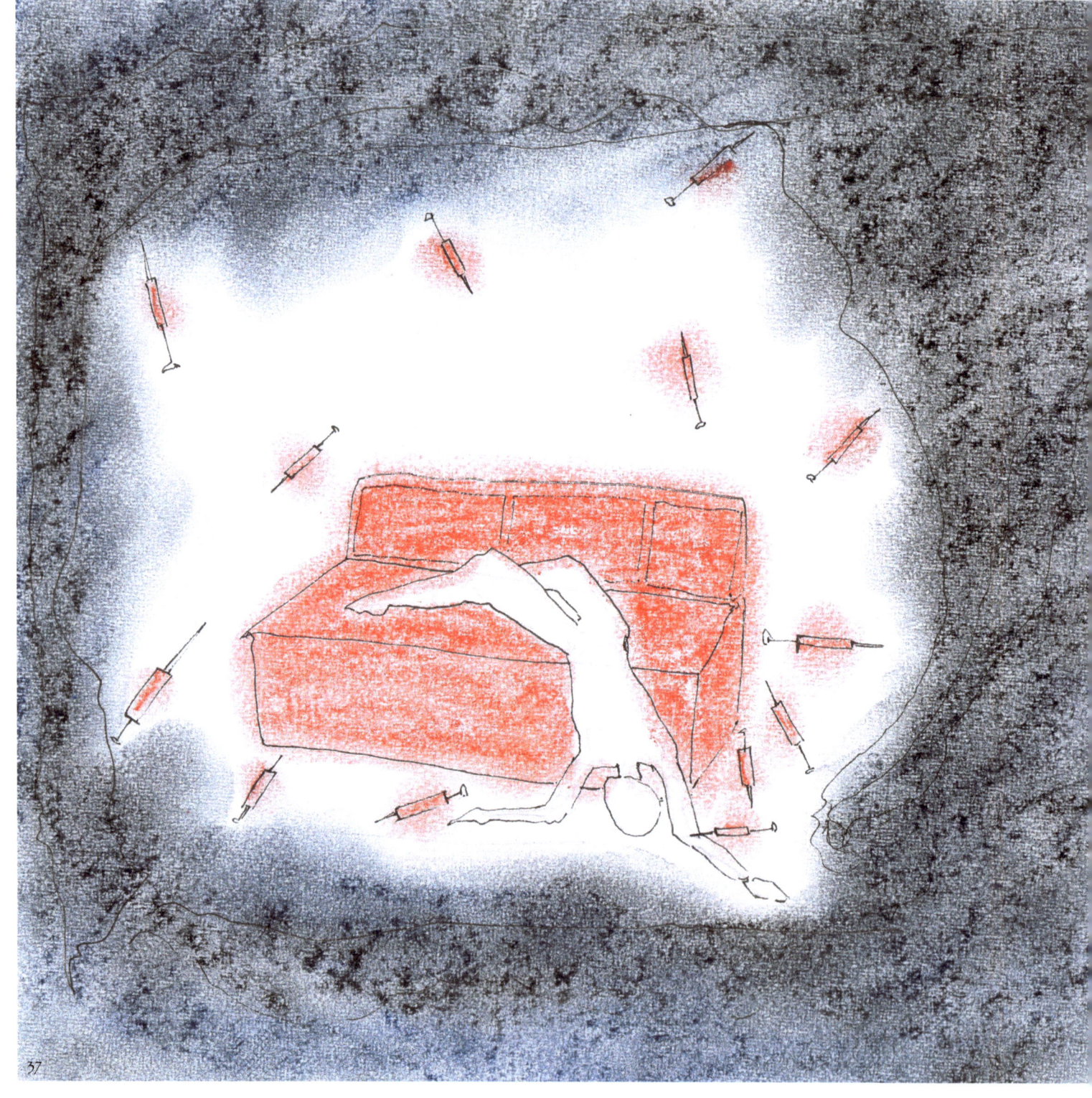

In the next chamber I only briefly stopped by, I knew I was running out of time. Another friend was lying there in a casual living room setting. Her eyes were blank and she was contorted awkwardly, lying half upside down off the sofa. There were needles all over the room and one in her arm. I was flooded with a memory of her colorful and warm apartment filled with vintage treasures, her and our other friend who had also died smoking a cigarette and listening to some obscure and wonderful music and watching a film about magic. I tucked it into my backpack and kept walking.

In the next chamber, I saw myself. I was shrunken and sickly, ashen blue in white with milky eyes like the rest of the dead I had visited. I stood in the middle of the room, still and erect with a demonic grin. I watched and at the same time was spontaneously consumed in fire and in the pillar of the flame I was jacketed in the old catholic school uniform I had been forced to wear, the white turtleneck strangling me. I was starting up at the dome ceiling of that whitewashed chapel, I was dead inside without realizing. Then I was consumed and crazed by the specter of my insane tormenter, her face layering over and into and controlling mine. I stood watching these fatal injuries happen to myself from the edge of the chamber. I realized I wasn't going to make it and tried to conjure memories of myself before these injuries happened to me.

39

On the burning pillar I piled and grew all of the stuff of the Earth that I had loved so much as a kid, the plants and animals, especially from the rainforest. And also heaps of color, paint and ink, all of my art materials and art explosions piled up to the sky. I drowned out the flame with color and the Earth. I saw myself as a laughing and silly kid. At this small triumph, the dead demonic me leapt out of the chamber, its eyes raging and black, its mouth inhumanly agape and large, teeming with the black chalken air of the underworld. It scurried in a disjointed and alien manner around the protector spirits where they couldn't quite see to get behind me and tapped me on the back, sniveling and chuckling demonically. The protector spirits jolted at my cry of fear into ferocious movements and snarled and snapped at the dead me, forcing it back into its chamber. Rattled and worried part of it had come into me when it touched me, I put the memories of color and the Earth into my backpack and continued on into the darkness.

At this point, I became aware of how long I had been down there and felt myself growing weak. No one else directly appeared to me but I thought of two more people in my life. I saw her isolated and alone in her house, pacing about trying to distract herself from her deep suffering and loneliness by cleaning and tending the garden. I was horrified as no memories flooded me of her, only beautifully wrapped and dazzling holiday boxes marked with her handwriting from far away. I instead tried to conjure a memory I would like to make with her and was flooded with an image of she and I surrounded by exotic plants in the conservatory in the park. I put this in my backpack and vowed to take her there over the holidays. I kept walking.

I then saw the other person I had thought of. She looked sickly and angular, alone, her extremities cold and blue. I was confronted with all the ways we may have unknowingly hurt each other, even though I had always tried to shield her from pain. But I was flooded with happy memories of decorating the house and doing festive activities over the holidays, they were the only safe times. We are cutting paper snowflakes and putting them in the window. We are watching the Snowman and making silly plays of modern holiday stories. And then, warm memories of all of us with her at the holidays, searching for our hidden easter baskets, finding Santa's beard in the fire grate, carving pumpkins, sitting by a glowing tree, walking into a room glittering with beautiful presents. I tucked all of these carefully into my backpack and turned back into the darkness.

I recounted over and over all of the memories I had collected in my backpack to make sure they were all there to take back to the land of the living. I promised all of the dead I had visited that I would keep the memories close to me and try my best to use them as best I could for our healing in the other world. With the protector spirits beside me, I closed my eyes. We didn't say good-bye. I could hear the dogs barking above me guiding me back to the land of living. I don't remember my climb out. I awoke in my tent wrapped in blankets, my friend's dog huddled against my legs, an impression of the stones pressed deep into my palms. There were still red fires glittering across the surface of the dark desert. I quietly cried myself to sleep.

I awoke the next morning and was told all of the dogs throughout the campsites howled together in unison at some point during the night, waking my friends. I did not know what I would do with the things I had brought back but I knew I had no choice but to start over.